The Mysterious Lumps in the Bed

ALAUNA BOYKIN

Illustrated by **JUDY GRUPP**

Dedicated to my friends and family
for their constant encouragement to continue to write.
Thank you for your faith in me.

This book has taken years to write because of several cats who insisted on helping by playing in the bed clothes. I often struggled to make the bed with all the "help" I received from my sweet furry friends under the sheets and covers.

I would start a story and then let it sit and then get it out again and again, trying to make it work as a book.

I finally figured it out!

ISBN 13: 978-1-64649-253-4

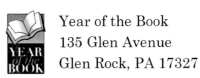
Year of the Book
135 Glen Avenue
Glen Rock, PA 17327

Lucy loves a good story.

Every night before she goes to sleep,
she sits on her bed
and reads a book from the library.
She really likes stories about
animals, dinosaurs, and mysteries.

Lucy fluffs up her super-big blue pillow
and gets comfortable.
She has a mystery book tonight
that she is excited to read.

She opens to the first page.

But then Lucy
notices something.

There is a mysterious lump
under the blanket
at the bottom of her bed.
The lump wanders back and forth
and inches its way toward her.

Up, up, up,
closer and closer
it comes.

"Stop, Lump!" Lucy says.

The lump stops.

**What is this lump,
and why is it in Lucy's bed?**

It's a mystery.

Lucy reaches out and touches the lump.
It's soft and not very large.

Hmm, she wonders,
could it be a cat size lump?

Lucy sings to the lump.

"There's a cat size lump
in my bed,
in my bed.
There's a cat size lump
in my bed.

Now, which is the tail
and which is the head
of the cat size lump
in my bed?

I give a little tickle.
It gives a little purr.
I wonder what it said!

There's a cat size lump
in my bed,
in my bed..."

"There's a cat size lump in my bed!"

"Okay now," she says to the lump.
"You have to leave because I want to read my book."

The lump slowly heads
to the bottom of the bed.
Then it jumps to the floor
and comes out from under the blanket.
It's Jack, Lucy's cat!
He has long black and white fur
and a large, fluffy tail.

"Go on, Jack," Lucy says. "Go downstairs."

He gives his tail a big swish and walks to her
bedroom door. But then he stops and,
in a clever kitty way, turns around as if to say,

"Okay, Lucy, thanks for the game.
Let's play again later."

For the second time,
Lucy fluffs up her super-big blue pillow
just right and gets comfortable.

Then she starts to read her mystery book again.

But wait a minute . . .

hold on . . .

not again!

There's another lump in her bed.
It's a medium size lump this time.
This lump is very wiggly,
and she wonders
if it could be a dog size lump.

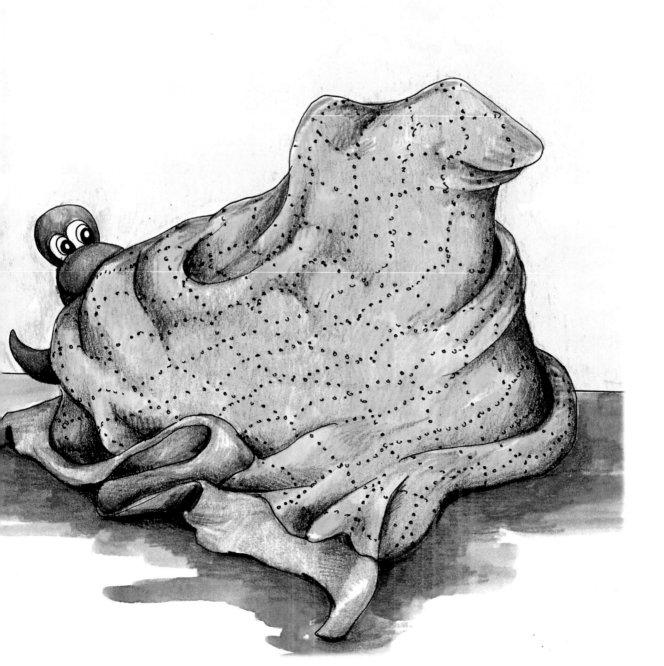

It's another
mystery.

Lucy sings,

"There's a dog size lump
in my bed,
in my bed.
There's a dog size lump in my bed.

Now, which is the tail
and which is the head
of the dog size lump in my bed?

I give a little tickle.
It gives a little woof.
I wonder what it said!

There's a dog size lump
in my bed,
in my bed..."

"There's a dog size lump in my bed."

"Stop, Lump!" Lucy says. The lump stops.
"Okay now. You have to leave
so I can read my book.

The lump circles around under the blanket,
then stops moving. It does not leave.

Lucy says to the lump,
"Go on, get out of here."

The lump slowly moves
toward the bottom of the bed.
It peeks out from under the blanket,
and Lucy sees it is Jade, her family dog.
Jade is a beautiful brown boxer pup.

"Go downstairs, Jade."

The playful puppy hops down
from under the blanket
and strolls toward the bedroom door.
But before she leaves, she turns around
in a sly doggie way.
She wags her stubby little tail,
and Lucy knows Jade is thinking,

"Okay, Lucy.
Thanks for the game.
Let's play again later."

For the third time,
Lucy fluffs up her super-big blue pillow
just right and starts to
read her book and . . .

Oh no! . . .

hold on . . .

what now?

She can't believe there's another lump in her bed!
It's a much larger lump this time.
It can hardly move around under the blanket.

It's not a cat size lump or a dog size lump.
What in the world could it be?

Could it possibly be a brother size lump?

Lucy sings,
"There's a brother size lump
in my bed,
in my bed.

There's a brother size lump
in my bed.

Now, which is the tail
and which is the head
of the brother size lump
in my bed?

I give a little tickle.
It gives a little laugh.
I wonder what it said!

There's a brother size lump
in my bed,
in my bed..."

"There's a brother size lump in my bed."

"Come out from under that blanket," Lucy says.
"I know who you are!"

The lump giggles.
The lump is her little brother, Sam.

"Come on, Sam.
I really want to read my book!"

Sam throws off the blanket
and sits up waving his arms and laughing.

He's having a very good time.

Lucy asks Sam,
"Do you want me to read my book to you?"

"Yes, yes!" he yells,
and crawls toward her and her pillow.

Lucy and Sam get comfortable
on her super-big blue pillow
and begin reading her book.

But they are only lump-free for a few minutes.
Soon all the lumps are back under the blanket
and creeping toward them.

So here they are...
Lucy, a cat, a dog, and a brother
all in one bed ready for a story.

*The mystery of
the lumps in the bed
is solved!*

And Lucy thinks it's good.
Do you know why?
She likes sharing her bed
with all those lumps!

Wouldn't you?

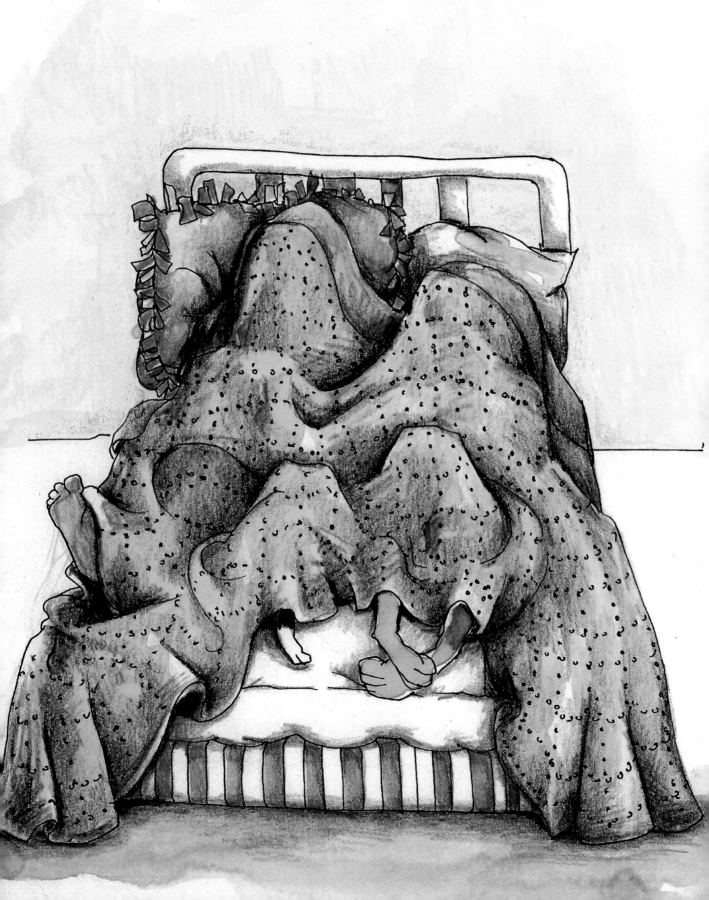

Alauna Boykin has always loved making up stories. She is an animal and bird lover but is especially drawn to children. She has twin granddaughters. These girls not only keep her on her toes but continue to stretch her imagination to places we all need to visit on a regular basis. Alauna is working on new book ideas, so watch for more storytelling soon.

Judy Grupp is an author/illustrator, a lover of whimsy, crayons and gummy bears. She draws and writes not only for kids but also for the young-at-heart. Judy has created more than a dozen books including: *The New Adventures of Jeremy Duck, Key Lime Lullaby, Gravy in the Graveyard,* and *Abby's Bedtime Story.*

Made in the USA
Middletown, DE
16 May 2022

65803474R00022